Peppa Pig™

Happy Easter

Sticker Activity Book

There's a special golden egg hiding somewhere in this book. Can you find it?

Answer: page 10

Spring Surprise

Peppa and George are visiting Granny and Grandpa Pig. They are going to have an Easter egg hunt! Colour in the excited piggies, then stick a yellow sun in the sky.

Hurry Up, Freddy!

Lots of Peppa's friends are coming to join in the fun. Everyone is here, apart from Freddy Fox. Put your finger on Mr Fox's van. Help him choose the road that leads to the Easter egg hunt.

B

C

A

Answer: road C

Stick and Share

Now that Freddy's here, the Easter egg hunt can begin. Use your stickers to give everyone a basket to hold.

Peppa

George

Rebecca

Emily

Freddy

Richard

Edmond

How many baskets did you give out? Write the number here.

Answer: 7 baskets

Flower Fun

There are lots of chocolate eggs hidden in the garden.
The children are allowed to go and find them, as long as they
don't step on Grandpa Pig's plants. Everybody is very careful.

Draw a pretty flower on each
of the stalks. There are lots of
new flowers in springtime!

Peppa's Easter Egg Hunt

Peppa and her friends start hunting for eggs. Come and hunt, too!
Search Grandpa Pig's garden, then stick a matching egg on top of
every one that you spot.

Can you
also find . . .   a snail   a watering can

a barbecue

Granny Pig's hat

Eggs for Everyone!

Wait a minute . . . not everybody has an egg!
What about the little ones? Grandpa Pig
makes sure that George, Richard and Edmond
get an egg, too. Add the missing sticker shapes
and finish off the picture.

Page 2

Page 4

Page 9

Page 8

Page 10

Pages 6-7

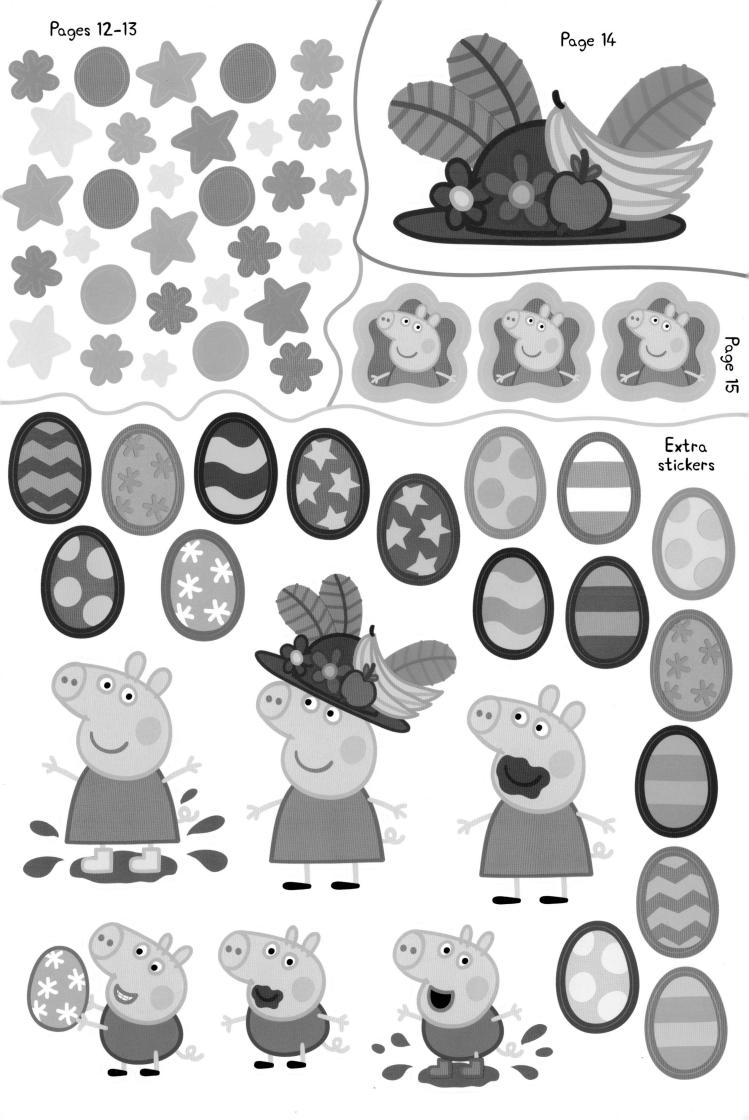

Pages 12–13

Page 14

Page 15

Extra stickers

Dot-to-Choc

Easter eggs are pretty and they taste scrummy, too!
Use your pencil or crayon to join up the dots,
then decorate this giant egg with colourful patterns.

Easter Chicks

Granny Pig has some news. George, Richard and Edmond are not going to be the littlest ones for much longer. Some chicks are coming!

Peep into Granny Pig's chicken house. What are about to hatch? Trace over the letters then put the matching sticker into the frame.

Find the sticker

chicks

Spot the Difference

Here come the baby chicks . . . one, two, three! Look at the pictures.
Can you spot three differences between them? Colour in a chick
each time you spot a difference.

Answers: 1. The black hen has moved from
the grass into the chicken house.
2. The brown hen is missing.
3. The sun has gone behind a cloud.

Make Your Own Spring Chick

It is very exciting when eggs start to hatch!
Make your own spring chick, then sing Peppa's song.

You will need:

Scissors
Glue
Cardboard
Plain card
A pencil
Crayons or colouring pencils
A split pin

Ask a grown-up
to help you!

"I'm a little chick singing, 'Cheep, cheep, cheep!'
I like to pick up food with my beak, beak, beak.
I've a fluffy yellow head and straw for my bed,
And I jump up and down singing, 'Cheep, cheep, cheep!'"

What to do:

1
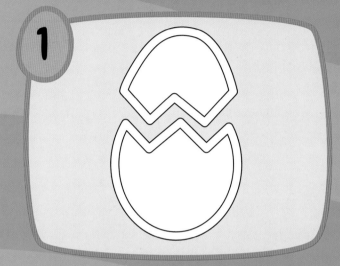

Trace these egg shapes on to a thin piece of cardboard and ask a grown-up to help you cut them out.

2

Use your crayons or colouring pencils to decorate them. You could add stickers, too!

3

Trace this chick on to a piece of plain card and colour it in. Then ask an adult to help you cut it out. Stick this to the bottom piece of the egg shape.

4

Carefully push the split pin through the very left corner of both egg shapes. Open it out and your chick is ready to hatch!

Peppa's Bonnet

Now the chicks have hatched, it really is springtime!
Peppa wants to wear her special spring bonnet.
Look at the hats, then stick the right one on to Peppa's head.

Spring Things

Something's not quite right in Grandpa Pig's garden. Put a Peppa Pig sticker on the things that don't belong outside on a sunny spring day. There are three to find.

Answers: 1. The snowman. 2. The grandfather clock. 3. The teapot.

Three Easter Cheers

What a fun spring day! Peppa gives three cheers to Granny and Grandpa Pig. Hip hip hooray! Draw a picture of yourself cheering, too.